MY FIRST LOOK AT HOLIDAYS

THANKSGIVING DAY CAN BE COLD

Thanksgiving

VALERIE BODDEN

CREATIVE EDUCATION

Published by Creative Education

123 South Broad Street, Mankato, Minnesota 56001

Creative Education is an imprint of The Creative Company

Designed by Rita Marshall

Photographs by Archive Photos, Getty Images (Paul & Lindamarie Ambrose, Steven W.

Jones), Donald Kelly, Gary Kelley, Bonnie Sue, Unicorn Stock Photos (Jean Higgins), Joe

Viesti, Donald Voelker

Cover illustration © 1996 Roberto Innocenti

Copyright © 2006 Creative Education

International copyright reserved in all countries.

No part of this book may be reproduced in any form without

written permission from the publisher.

Printed in the United States of America

Library of Congress Cataloging-in-Publication Data

TO COME

First edition 9 8 7 6 5 4 3 2 1

Thanksgiving

Being Thankful

Thanksgiving is a **holiday** for giving thanks. To "give thanks" means to say "Thank you." On Thanksgiving, people give thanks for their family and friends. They give thanks for their home and their life.

People celebrate Thanksgiving in fall because fall is **harvest** time. Farmers pick a lot of fruits and vegetables in fall. People give thanks for all their food on Thanksgiving.

The world's biggest
pumpkin pie weighed
more than 350 pounds (159 kg).

In the United States, Thanksgiving comes at the end of November. It is always on a Thursday. In Canada, Thanksgiving comes at the beginning of October. It is always on a Monday.

An Old Holiday

In 1578, an English **explorer** landed in Canada. He gave thanks for his safe trip across the ocean. And he celebrated with a big meal called a feast. This was the first Thanksgiving in Canada.

PILGRIMS CAME TO AMERICA ON SHIPS LIKE THIS

In 1621, people called "pilgrims" came to America from England. Life was hard for the pilgrims, but **Native Americans** helped them. They showed the pilgrims how to plant fruits and vegetables.

The pilgrims had a lot of food that year. They were thankful, so they had a feast. They asked many Native Americans to eat with them. Then everybody played games. The first Thanksgiving in America lasted three days.

The pilgrims did not use forks.

They ate with spoons,

knives, and their fingers.

Family and Food

Thanksgiving is a day for family. Some people travel far to spend Thanksgiving with their families. Most kids do not have school on Thanksgiving. Many grown-ups do not have to work.

Many families have Thanksgiving **traditions**. Some families go to church. Some watch football. Others go to parades.

The world's biggest turkey
weighed 86 pounds (39 kg).
That is as big as a large dog!

Thanksgiving is a day for food! Most people eat turkey. They may have bread and potatoes, too. Some people make stuffing and vegetables. Pumpkin pie is a popular dessert. Some of these foods were eaten at the first Thanksgiving.

Some people call

Thanksgiving "Turkey Day"

because so many

people eat turkey.

MACY'S THANKSGIVING DAY PARADE IN NEW YORK

MORE THANKSGIVING FUN

New York City has a special Thanksgiving tradition called the "Macy's Thanksgiving Day Parade." There are many huge balloons in the parade. The balloons are shaped like cartoon characters.

Many people decorate their houses for Thanksgiving. One special decoration is called a "cornucopia." A cornucopia is a

Leaves change color before Thanksgiving

basket shaped like a horn. It is filled with fruit and other foods.

Many people get ready for Christmas on the day after Thanksgiving. Some people go shopping. Some people rest and relax. At the end of the day, there is usually leftover turkey to eat!

Some people snap

a wishbone from a turkey

for good luck.

A CORNUCOPIA FILLED WITH FRUITS AND VEGETABLES

Hands-on: A Thankful Tree

Make a "Thankful Tree" to show all the things you are thankful for!

What You Need

Construction paper of all colors

Crayons

Scissors

Glue

What You Do

1. Trace your hand on at least six sheets of construction paper.
2. Have a grown-up help you cut out the handprints.
3. Write something you are thankful for on each hand-print.
4. Draw a tree trunk and branches on a sheet of brown construction paper. Have a grown-up help you cut out the tree.
5. Glue the handprints onto the tree like leaves.

GRAND DINNER
IN HONOR OF

Thanksgiving

THE LAST
THURSDAY
IN NOVEMBER

Soup

CREAM OF PLENTY

Entree

TURKEY - YOUNG AND
TENDER

SPARKLING WATER

Vegetables

CABBAGE
AMPLE

GOOD OLD CIDER

POTATOES-
SWEET

A THANKSGIVING MEAL TO BE THANKFUL FOR

Index

Words to Know

explorer—a person who goes to a new place to find new things

harvest—the time of year when farmers pick plants from their fields

holiday—a special day that happens every year

Native Americans—the first people who lived in America; they are also called Indians

traditions—things that people do every year

Read More

Haugen, Brenda. *Thanksgiving*. Minneapolis, Minn.: Picture Window Books, 2004.

Klingel, Cynthia, and Robert B. Noyed. *Thanksgiving*. Chanhassen, Minn.: The Child's World, 2003.

Rosinsky, Natalie M. *Thanksgiving*. Minneapolis, Minn.: Compass Point Books, 2003.

Explore the Web

Billy Bear's Happy Thanksgiving

http://www.billybear4kids.com/holidays/thanksgiving/thanksgiving.htm

BlackDog's Thanksgiving Fun and Games

http://blackdog.net/holiday/thanks/index.html

Thanksgiving at PrimaryGames.com

http://www.primarygames.com/holidays/thanksgiving/thanksgiving.htm